ROBIN HOD

BY BRIAN VINCENT

DEDICATED TO

CHARLES HENRY VINCENT

Copyright © Brian Vincent 2017

Best wishes

Brian Vincent

INTRODUCTION

There have been many films made and books written regarding Englands colourful and sometimes turbulent history. There have always been two questions I have always asked myself. How do we know for sure that certain events have been recorded correctly and how can we distinguish between fact and fiction ? For example, is the spelling correct in the recorded reports, as just one spelling mistake may throw a whole new light on what had accurately taken place. A good example of this relates to Sir Francis DrakeWe have always been told and we have always believed that Sir Francis Drake had been playing a game of bowls as he was informed that the Spanish Armada was sailing towards the south coast of England. This account is just totally wrong and untrue and came about because of just one spelling mistake. What really happened was that Drake was taking his dog for a walk along the cliff tops of the south coast, when just on the horizon he spotted the Spanish Armada. He was not playing a game of bowls but his bowels were playing up. As would anybodies who had just seen the whole Spanish fleet sailing towards the south coast of England with all guns blazing. The incorrect spelling of just one word had thrown a new light on what had actually taken place. Yet another example and which has nothing to do with spelling mistakes, as the event had just been incorrectly recorded, relates to Sir Walter Raleigh. It is said that Sir Walter Raleigh had set sail for the new world where he discovered the humble potato. Once again this account is totally untrue and just pure fabrication, which had probably been made up by someone with a wild and vivid imagination. Indeed, Raleigh had set sail for the new world, but just off shore an almighty storm blew up which forced raleigh to take shelter in Cardiff Bay. The storm raged on for over three days. Raleigh had decided to take full advantage of the situation. He decided to visit his sick Aunt who lived on the outskirts of Cardiff, and who was suffering from a rare and incurable disease known as Taffyitis. A condition caused by picking leeks in damp weather. It was while he was returning to his ship and to set sail for the new world that he discovered the humble potato in a Cardiff fish and chip shop. I could go on with a lot more examples but I feel I have made my point with the above two. What I really want to do now is to concentrate on the story of Robin Hood. Or to be more precise and accurate, Robin Hod. In the following pages I will tell the true story of this colourful and charismatic character from the depths of English history. His association with Richard The Lion Heart, the fall out with Prince John and the Sheriff of Nottingham, the many friends and associates he made on his travels such as Fryer tuck, who had nothing to do with monks from Fountains Abbey in North Yorkshire, Little John, who was not a giant of a man with the strength of a bull. But a small dwarf, who was covered in bruises due to getting under peoples feet during happy hour. Ivanhoe, a Welsh guy from the Rhonda in Wales, and Alan A

Dale, another Welsh guy who always kept up to date with the latest fashion and was well known for being a flamboyant dresser. Some people called him the original welsh dresser. You will read more on these characters and many more within the forth coming pages.

Robin Hood is one of the most famous stories in English history. But was he myth, legend, or fact ? Did he really live in Sherwood Forest with his band of merry men ? Did he rob from the rich and gave to the poor ? Or was he some kind of medieval Raffles, who robbed from the rich and kept it ? Many films have been made, together with plays and books that have been written regarding this colourful character from the depths of medieval England. But is there any truth in the story. I have already given an example in my introduction of how stories and reports can be distorted from the truth. The story and legend of Robin Hood is just one of these stories. The truth is that Robin Hood never existed. The stories and tales of an outlaw living in Sherwood Forest with his band of merry men, all dressed in Lincoln green and swinging from the trees like a medieval Tarzan is actually based on another colourful character who lived around the same period. But his name was Robin Hod. Robin Hod was a master builder and champion hod carrier. He was well known for charging high prices for the work he carried out. This gives us the name Robin. The name Hod speaks for it,s self. Although he was brought up in Nottingham, he carried out much of his work in London. New Cross to be exact. Nothing is known of his earlier years in Nottingham. But the story really starts in London, where he hung out with Richard the 1st, better known as Richard The Lion Heart. Richard, who was a keen dart player and lager lout played for the same two dart teams as Robin, the Red Lion and the White Heart public houses. This gives us the name Lion and Heart. The name by which Richard was better known. Although Richard was a poor dart player, he was very keen and the lads in the team loved him,as they could always rely on him for a small loan on match night. It was while playing for these two teams that Richard and Robin met for the very first time. They got on well together and became more like brothers rather than King and subject. It was while competing in an away dart match in France, which ended in defeat again, that trouble broke out. The story goes that Richard and Robin had lost touch with the rest of the lads so they made their way back to Calais to catch a ferry back home to Dover. Apparently, they had over two hours to wait, so they headed for the nearest tavern. It was in this tavern that an almighty bar room brawl broke out which involved Richard, Robin, and some of the local lads. The exact reason for the brawl is unknown but the blame was put on Richard. He was quickly arrested and charged with disorderly conduct and criminal damage. A charge which he strongly denied. The landlord of the tavern, who was a reasonable man, said he would drop all charges if Richard would pay for the damage, which included two chairs, a table, two or three dinted tankards and a broken window. Neither Richard or Robin could come up with the money as they had just spent their last French franc on two flagons of lager. Richard was taken into custody and was told that he would be released once the damage had been paid for. I would like to point out here that it was Calais that Richard was taken prisoner and not in Austria which is stated in the history books. Robin was released without charge and headed back to England to ask Prince John for the money so that Richard could be released. Robin boarded the next ferry and was soon back on English soil. Although feeling a little green around the gills, as the crossing was a little rough. The captain of the ferry had already told Robin to have a large bowl of porridge before setting sail. "Will that stop the sea sickness" Enquired Robin."No" replied the captain"But it will taste the same coming up as it does going down Now Prince John was well known for being a bit tight with his money. And let,s face it, he had plenty of it. One rummer that was going round at the time was that while he was visiting the local market, an old beggar had stumbled in front of him, which resulted in the old beggar tearing half the sole off his shoe. Prince John looked down at the old man who was dressed in rags and who did not have two groats to rub together, and produced a large leather purse from his pocket which was bursting at the seems, as it was stuffed full of gold and silver coins. He untied the string from it and handed it to the old beggar saying. " That should hold it together for a while"

Robin eventually arrived at Prince Johns castle and told him of what had happened back in France. On hearing the story, Prince John refused to cough up the money to free Richard. He shrugged his shoulders and turned to Robin saying."It,s got nowt to do with me"It was at this point that Robin had noticed a damp patch in the corner of the room. Never letting a chance slip by, Robin told Prince John that he could solve the problem. Anyway, the money which he received from fixing the problem would free Richard. Prince John agreed and Robin started work on it the very next day. The work was completed on schedule and Robin handed Prince John the bill, who soon started to shout and rave at Robin and an almighty argument ensued which nearly came to blows being struck. Prince John had the final word on the matter saying."Sod off you robbing git, you,l get nowt" Robin was branded a cowboy builder and not an outlaw as we have been led to believe. Prince John had Robin thrown out of the federation of master builders, as well as the castle.

Meanwhile, back in France, Richard had been released from custody after being bound over to keep the peace by a French magistrate. He was given the ferry fare home and a little money for food. With money in his pocket and a tremendous thirst raging, Richard headed for the nearest tavern. It was in this French tavern and after consuming his eighth flagon of lager that yet another bar room brawl broke out. The cause of it is unknown. Richard,s head had come into contact with an empty light ale bottle during the mayhem. Which did not seem that light at the time. Richard dropped to the floor like a lead balloon. On coming too, Richard had no recollection of who he was, where he was, or where he was going. With no more money in his pocket he wandered the streets of Calais in a dazed and confused state. He was eventually found by a cross dressing tap dancing instructor who went by the name of Pierre De Feet, who felt sorry for Richard and took him under his wing so to speak. Pierre taught Richard a few steps of dance. After much practice, Richard became quiet an accomplished dancer. He was that good that he ended up in a famous Parisian night club. Where he found work as a tap dancer and drag artist, performing twice nightly to a rapturous applause. He went by the stage name of Larry La Rue.

Now it was about this time that tales were being told of a grand scheme being planned in Scotland by a bright spark called Kenneth Mc Alpine. A few years earlier, he had been elected leader of the pics. His claim to fame though was bringing a tribe of Irish immigrants over from Ireland. These guys had broad shoulders and gigantic hands and could dig with a shovel all day long without breaking sweat. It was Mc Alpines plan that these guys would work alongside the Pics as they put Mc Alpines grand plan into operation. The two tribes got on well together and were later known as the Pic and Shovel brigade. It was McAlpines grand plan to join together the Irish and North sea by means of a canal, which is known today as the Caledonian Canal. Now I know what you are all asking. "Was it not Thomas Telford (1803-1823) who built the Caledonian Canal ? My answer is yes, but he only built the end bits. The middle bit known as Loch Ness was dug out by that great engineer, visionary and bright spark, Kenneth McAlpine and his Pic and Shovel brigade. One of the many mysteries which surround Loch Ness, is why part of it known as Urquart Bay is so wide and over 1,000 feet deep ? Two theories have been put forward regarding this mystery. The first one is that the Pic and Shovel brigade were habitual diggers that they got carried away with their work. The second theory is that Kenneth McAlpine lost a penny down a rabbit hole. The first theory is more plausible. Robin had heard of this grand scheme being planned through his building connections. With no one wanting to employ him in fear of upsetting Prince John, he set off on the long trek to Scotland along the Great North Road in search of McAlpines plc, where he hoped to find work. Nothing is known of Robins journey until he reaches Scotch Corner. Two suggestions have been put forward regarding this. The first is that Robin stole a horse and rode there. The second is that Robin took part in a few unauthorised house clearances to finance his journey. Neither of these suggestions ring true, as Robin was not that kind of person, and would have been totally out of character. However, there is evidence to to suggest that he applied his trade as a builder and took on odd jobs before word spread that he had been branded a cowboy builder by Prince John. Story,s have been told of a family in North Yorkshire called the Mintons, where Robin did do a couple of odd jobs. Now Mrs Minton had just lost her husband a couple of years earlier, and was finding it very difficult to bring up two unruly twin boys. The story goes that one morning, Mrs Minton had found the pet budgie stone cold dead at the bottom of it,s cage. She picked it up and walked to the back door, where one of the twins was playing in the garden, the other had gone over the fence at the bottom of the garden and was playing in a field. Mrs Minton threw the dead budgie to the nearest twin and asked him to bury it. He picked up a stick and knocked it over the fence to his twin brother, stating that it was his pet and that he should be the one to bury it. The other twin picked up a stick and knocked the budgie back, saying that it was his mother who had asked him to bury it. This went on for about five minutes. Mrs Minton arrived at the back door to see what all the commotion was. After seeing for herself what was happening she shouted at the two boys saying.

"your bad Mintons" And so the game of badminton was born.

Now We have all been led to believe that Fryer Tuck was a travelling monk from Fountains Abbey in North Yorkshire. It is said that he was resting under a tree in Sherwood Forest where Robin came across him and forced him to piggy back him across a small stream. Once again this tale is just pure fabrication. Tucks real name was Hamish Tucker. Fryer Tuck was just his nickname, as he was the proprietor of a small transport cafe, somewhere near Scotch Corner on the Great North Road. It was known locally as the Greasy Spoon. He had nothing to do with monks. Especially those from Fountains Abbey, who were the medieval equivalent of the modern day hoody, as they would lay in wait for the unsuspecting traveler and relieve them of their purse. The only link which Tuck had with monks, is that he did have a funny kind of hairstyle with a wider than normal parting, caused by a one of his chip pans catching fire. He got the nickname Fryer Tuck because most everything that he cooked was fried. Tuck was a plump guy who would fly into a rage if anyone criticised unhygienic ways. Local people would often say that you could always tell what Tuck was cooking because more often than not he would be wearing it. (no need for a menu then) Tuck was once blamed for a bad outbreak of salmonella and botulism which was due to his unhygienic ways. It was said that he had been informed by the health authority by letter to clean up his act. Tuck had always denied ever receiving such a letter. He had always maintained that the health authority always sent their letters by second class pigeon post. These pigeons were a lot slower that the pigeons they used for first class post. He claimed that the slower pigeons made an easy target and was probably shot down by an over enthusiastic grouse shooter who had mistaken it for a grouse. After all, it was the middle of the grouse shooting season when the letter was sent. Tuck got away with it and the greasy spoon remained open, even though he had a dustbin outside which had ulcers. His signature dish was frogs legs. But this did not go down well with his customers for two reasons. The first reason is that they did not like them and the second reason was that they kicked the chips off the plate. It was said that one customer complained to Tuck regarding the frog legs kicking the chips off the plate and was quickly thrown through an unopened window by Tuck. Yet another customer was given the same treatment for complaining that his side salad was on the wrong side of his plate. It was in this greasy spoon that Robin and Tuck met for the very first time.

Robin walked in and sat down on one of the bar stools.

"A flagon of tea and a bacon butty which you seem to be wearing" said Robin. Tuck turned round and looked Robin up and down. "Not from round here are you" enquired Tuck. "come up from London to find this bright spark called McAlpine" replied Robin. "Long way to go yet, you will need more than a bacon butty" laughed Tuck. Who placed a bacon butty on the counter and charged for two, quickly followed by a flagon of hot steaming tea. The two were soon in deep conversation discussing darts and near misses, which was a little unusual for Tuck as he did not take to strangers as they may be from the public health department. All of a sudden the door slammed with an almighty bang. Which shook the whole building and nearly took the door off the hinges. "Sorry about that but I have just had one hell of a day" Robin turned to see who had just walked in. It was Will scarlet, better known in his day as Scarlet Willy. Due to some form of social disease which he had picked up while working as a travelling pork pie salesman for Hadrian Walls and co. He was of medium build with a well weathered face and flat feet, due to the many miles he had travelled applying his trade. The problem was that he had just received a letter by first class pigeon post informing him that due to the fall in pork pie sales he was now redundant. The thing was that by the time Will Scarlet got the samples of pork pies to his potential customers, they were off. In fact they were rancid and the filling had turned green. Nobody wanted them. Even the local children had made up a rhyme.

"The dogs would not eat, the green meat, in the street""It does not surprise me that they do not keep in this weather, we are in the middle of a heat wave" remarked Tuck."So what are you going to do now" was Tucks next question."well there is no work round here, not with this recession, and I have just heard that it is going to get worse. One of the big banks have just gone down, Northern Brick""This guy has come up from London to seek work with McAlpine" remarked Tuck."Why not throw your lot in with him and go up to Inverness together" said Tuck."why not, safer travelling in numbers" said Robin."Good idea" said Will.Tuck made them up a batch of haggis sandwiches to eat on their way and again charged for two. Both thanked Tuck and set off on the Great North Road to Inverness to seek out this bright spark McAlpine.It was a hot and sticky afternoon as the two weary travellers came across two odd looking guys resting under a tree near a small burn. They too had heard of McAlpine but had been refused work and were on their way back home. McAlpine had heard of their reputation and did not want anyone upsetting his workforce. They were from a tribe of people who had settled in Wessex a couple of centuries ago and were known as Wazzocks. They were all over six feet tall, hence the saying we still use today. You great big Wazzock. They were an argumentative race of people who would argue with anyone on any subject, always thinking that they were right and everyone else was wrong. If you told a Wazzock that the grass was green he would argue all day with you and insist that it was blue. As Robin and Will got closer, they could hear the two Wazzocks arguing with each other over sometriviality.

"Good day to you" said Robin."What,s good about it" replied the biggest Wazzock of the two."Well, the sun is shining and the bird,s are singing and we are on our way to Scotland" replied Robin."Aye, and it,s all up hill from Wessex""That,s right, but it,s all down hill going back"There's logic there thought Will, who nodded in agreement. The great big Wazzock was furious, as nobody has ever been known to have won an argument with a Wazzock before. Red in the face and steam coming from his ears the Wazzock got to his feet and threw an almighty punch at Robin which luckily missed. Although he could have caught a nasty cold from the draft it created. Robin retaliated by giving him a swifty kick in the Urals and Trossachs, depending which part of the world you are in at the time. The Wazzock fell to the ground like a medieval sack of King Edwards, as Robin and Will legged it up the road, trying to put as much distance between them. The other Wazzock, who was more concerned about his friend rather than trying to catch Robin and Will, helped him to his feet. All the colour had drained from his face and with blood shot eyes could just about   see Robin and Will disappear over the horizon, as he waved his fists in the air and shouted a few choice words in a few octaves higher than he did before.

Meanwhile, back in a famous Parisian nightclub, Richard was still tapping away twice nightly to a rapturous applause. The French people loved him as they flocked in their thousands to see him perform. He had become quite a celebrity with his fancy frocks and tap dancing skills. Back in England, Prince John had one hand firmly placed on the English crown. However, he was becoming a little worried. People were starting to ask questions as to Richards whereabouts. All kinds of rumours were beginning to circulate as to Richards whereabouts so Prince John started a rumour of his own. The story goes that Richard had decided to travel to the middle east to open a string of corner shops with his business partner, a Mr Patel. It was while working late stock tacking, that he was hit and killed by ram raiders. The problem was that Robin was the only person who knew of Richards true whereabouts and if he talked, then the game would be up. Not only that, but the damp patch had returned on the castle wall. Prince John had wanted posters made up by his scribes and circulated throughout the land. They stated that Robin was wanted for tax evasion and offered a reward for information leading to his arrest. Someone somewhere must know of his whereabouts. He also thought that the reward money would help jog some ones memory too. After all, the country had just gone into a recession and as I have already mentioned earlier. Northern Brick had just gone down.

Back on the Great North Road, Robin and Will had just about caught their breath after their encounter with the two big Wazzocks from Wessex. The two rested for a while before continuing on their journey north. It was now late in the day and the sun was just about to set. As daylight turned into twilight, the two weary travellers thoughts turned to where they were going to spend the night. Their eyes scoured the landscape, looking for a distant light from a remote farm house which may offer shelter for the night. Nothing could be seen. The situation was getting worse as the wind was picking up and the scotch mist started to roll down the glens. Then, just as the two went over the brow of a hill, they thought they could see a glimmering light in the distance. The two headed straight for it. Robin and Will picked up a little more speed and soon reached their destination. They soon realised that the light was from a quaint little tavern called The Sporran Makers Arms.

The Sporran Makers Arms was one of those taverns which reminded Robin of the taverns back in England. Two of the windows was boarded up due to the previous night,s bar room brawl. As the two entered the tavern, Robins eyes were transfixed on a rather buxom woman who was just in the process of throwing out another drunk by the scruff of the neck.

"Serving wench" shouted Robin.
"Two flagons of heavy please"
"I,m no serving wench, I,m a barmaid" she replied.
"What,s your name barmaid"
"Marion" she said.
"Well then maid Marion, two flagons of heavy, and give the little guy one too, he looks like he could do with one"

Sat in the corner was a little guy of around four feet tall and he looked really cheesed off. He was covered in bruises due to getting under peoples feet during happy hour. "Be careful of him" said Marion.
"He can be very nasty when he,s had a few. Especially when he drinks shorts"

The little guy jumped from his buffet and joined Robin and Will at a table. He now looked very chuffed, as nobody had ever bought him a drink before. He introduced himself as Little John.
"Fancy a game of dominoes" He asked.
"No thanks, I can,t throw doms" replied Robin.
The two were soon in deep discussion about darts as Will ordered another three flagons of heavy, which was brought over to the table by Marion.

I would now like to mention something here, that not many people know about. It is one of the most important and significant incidents that had occurred in Scottish history. I am of course referring to the collapse and disbandment of the Scottish theatre industry. Most people do not realise that the majority of the play,s scripts were regarded as lost or destroyed. In actual fact, they were discovered hundreds of years later. Most of the titles and storyline had been changed, as they were made into films by Hollywood. Great works like, A Rebel With A Cause, The Italian Falcon, The Front Window, South By South East, And one of the best ever plays to come out of Scotland. Hamlet And Castella by Henry Winterman. It was in this industry that Little John tried to make his mark in life. He started out at an early age as a trainee stuntman. After being thrown off cliffs, fired from canons, thrown through unopened windows, kicked, punched and generally abused, he turned to acting. The problem with this was his size. Because of this he was only offered small parts. He was once put on a short list of two to play the leading roll in that great play, A Midsummer Nightmare, but the other guy got the part. The industry started to decline due to bad acting and an even worse critic. Another factor which played a major roll in the industries decline was the general public. They would rather turn up on a Saturday afternoon to watch the catholics and protestants kick seven bells out of each other for forty five minutes each way, with the promise of a marching band at half time, consisting of two guys playing the bagpipes and another knocking hell out of a big drum. I am referring of course to the Celtic versus Rangers match, which always drew in the crowds. Little John had tried many jobs after the decline of the theatre industry. Ferret breeder, whippet trainer, taxidermist where he specialised in haggis. He was a complete failure in everything he tried. It was at this point that Little John took to the bottle. On just one occasion, he found himself in front of the local magistrate on a charge of drunk and disorderly conduct. "This is not the first time you have been before me" said the magistrate. "And I don,t think it will be the last" mumbled Little John under his breath. "because you seem to enjoy being behind bars, I will put you behind some for three month,s. Maybe that will put you back on your feet" "I can do three month,s standing on my head" shouted Little John" "then you can do another three month,s to get you on your feet again" was the reply. It was while Little John was drowning his sorrows in the Sporran Makers Arms after being released and pouring out his sorrows to Maid Marion, that she felt sorry for the little guy and offered him employment as a tankard collector and washer up. He told Robin and Will the whole story, only pausing to order another three flagons of heavy. All of a sudden, the tavern door flung open and in walked a smartly dressed guy wearing some rather flamboyant clothes. It was Alan A Dale.

Alan A Dale was a singer, song writer, travelling minstrel and Welshman from the Rhonda Valley in Wales. (just thought I would mention that just in case you did not know where the Rhonda Valley was) He was very much into the fashion of the day and always dressed in the most flamboyant clothes when performing. Many people said that he was the original Welsh dresser, he was once in trouble for wearing a loud shirt in a public place. He spoke with a higher than normal pitched voice and if he lived in the modern times he would be catching the other bus, or batting for the other side. I think you know what I mean. Marion brought him over to the table where Robin, Will Scarlet and Little John were sitting and introduced him, stating that he would be doing a gig at the Sporran Makers Arms the very next night and hoped that everyone would stay to see him perform.

"I should have known you were from Wales by your funny accent" said Little John."You guys from down there have always amazed me. If you are not playing snooker or darts you are always singing. What the heck you have to sing about beats me"

"It,s alright" said Robin. "The little chap means no harm"Alan A Dale just looked down at Little John and forced a smile."That,s alright boyo" replied Alan A Dale in his feminine voice.Little John turned to Robin and said quietly."You know, I just can not put my finger on it but there is something odd about him"Just then, a tremendous blast on a buffalo horn was heard, which shook the tavern."Time gentlemen please" shouted Marion.As she gave yet another great blast on the buffalo horn "I can let you lads stay hear for the night if you want but I only have one spare room upstairs and Alan has already booked it in advance. However, it does have a double bed in it and if Alan does not mind sharing it with one of you, then I don,t mind"I don,t mind at all boyo"said Alan A Dale, as he looked the three lads up and down with a hint of a sparkle in his eye and a wider than normal grin on his face. For some strange reason the three lads declined the offer and opted to stay in the bar, where a log fire was still ablaze, and with that said, everyone retired for the night. The rain was lashing down and the wind was howling down the chimney as a great storm was raging outside. But it was warm and cosy in the tavern as the lads slept on undisturbed. Not even Little Johns stomach, which rumbled on well into the night could disturb anyone. It was just before dawn when the silence was broken and which woke everyone apart from Little John, who could sleep through a herd of elephnts stampeding through the tavern.

"**FIRE, FIRE. THE PLACE IS ON FIRE**" Shouted Robin.

Who leapt to his feet to find the whole tavern full of smoke and Little John still fast asleep and smouldering behind the tavern bar. The problem was that Little John had developed a liking for the odd Rastafairian Old Holborn and had smoked one earlier on in the night. He had fallen asleep and had dropped the tab end which was still alight and which started a small fire right next to a bottle of the finest Saudi Arabian brandy. Robin grabbed a bucket of water from behind the bar which was kept there for such a purpose and which Marion was compelled to do, as there were very strict health and safety laws in place at that particular time. He threw the water including the bucket over Little John which put him out in more ways than one. Robin thought that he had done him serious harm, as the bucket hit him on the head with tremendous force, but Little John was a tough little chap and was soon on his feet shouting and screaming at the top of his voice.

"What,s up, what,s up" he yelled.

"And why am I all wet" he screamed.

"You have just set the place on fire" shouted Robin.

"You must be dreaming" Replied Little John.

"Then what's all this smoke"

"Er, umm, I, er, Scotch mist" Said Little John.

It was at this point that Marion appeared on the scene, followed by Alan A Dale, who had been woken from their sleep by the noise and had come down stairs to see what all the commotion was all about. Just then, a loud explosion was heard coming from the cellar. A full barrel of rum had just exploded and which had just been imported from Bahrain. Everyone ran outside before the whole place went up like a furnace. Marion was in tears as she had lost everything in the fire. Alan A Dale was close to tears too, as he had lost all his designer cloths to the flames. Including his prize possession, his pink blazer.

As the sun came up and the flames went down, all five could only stare at the pile of smoldering ash that was once the Sporran Makers Arms. There was only one thing to do. Robin suggested that all five should travel together along the Great North Road to seek out Kenneth Mc Alpine plc in the hope of finding work, and with that, all five set off for Inverness. Their attention was soon turned to where they were going to spend the night, as it was getting late in the day and the five had been walking for miles. Only stopping for Marion to catch her breath. Little Johns stomach had started to rumble too, which meant only one thing. It was well past tea time.

"Listen boyo" Said Alan A Dale.

"I know of a boarding house not far from here. It,s a bit rough but it,s the only place for miles" The other four agreed. They had walked around six more miles when in the distance the boarding house came into view. It was just as Alan A Dale had said it would be. Rough."We can,t stay there" Remarked Will Scarlet."The place looks infested"Said Marion. Little John just stared opened mouthed as he eyed the place up and down. The boarding house was one of those places where you wiped your feet before you left, even the rats were running around in overalls and the mice were throwing themselves on the traps."Sorry boyo, but it,s the only place for miles" said Alan A Dale once again."We have to stay somewhere" said Robin,"And it,s going to be a cold night""Well, I suppose it is only for the one night" remarked Marion. Everyone agreed to risk it for just the one night. Robin went up to the door and after a few loud knocks on the door, it was opened by the proprietor and mine host, Big Brenda. Robin took a few paces back and just looked at Big Brenda in complete amazement, just not believing in what he was seeing. Little John ran for cover as he did in any crisis, and believe me, this was a crisis. To say that Big Brenda was a large woman would be an understatement. She was around six feet tall and must have weighed well over forty stone. Her arms and shoulders resembled those of a Russian shot putter with a face to match. She was cross eyed with one eye being larger than the other. Her legs were like tree trunks and covered in varicose veins. In fact

to look at her legs would be like looking at a modern day road map of the British Isles. She even wore a pair of heavy duty braces to hold her thong up. She was the kind of woman that you would take round the tunnel of love in a speedboat, providing you wanted to take her round in the first place. The whole glen was cast in shadow as she took a step forward across the thresh hold and eyed the weary travellers up and down.
"Well, what do you want at this time of night" She screamed.
"Er, well, I, mmm, er"
"Well, what is it" She screamed again.
Robin was lost for words. Never in his wildest dreams had he seen such a monster, although he had read of them. She was covered from head to foot in little round bruises, where people had pushed her away with ten foot barge poles.
"Well, speak up, what do you want"
"Well, er, I was wondering, I mean we were wondering if you had a room for the night" Enquired Robin.
"Just the one night" she bellowed.
"That,s right, just the one night" replied Robin.
The others just nodded in agreement.

"No one ever stops for more than the one night" she muttered under her breath. "Not surprised" whispered Little John. Big Brenda threw open the door and invited the weary travellers in. Then, finally slammed it shut with an almighty bang. Locked it, bolted it, chained it and finally padlocked it. She did not want any of her guests leaving in the middle of the night. Especially if they had not paid. She then proceeded to take her guests into the front room where she laid down the house rules yet again. The boarding house reminded Will Scarlet of home. Filthy and full of strangers. **"I RUN A VERY STRICT BOARDING HOUSE"** She screamed."**NO CHILDREN, NO DOGS, NO CATS AND EVEN THE RATS HAVE TO SIGN THE POISON BOOK, AND I AINT COOKING ANY FOOD AT THIS TIME OF NIGHT"** She bellowed. "That,s alright, we were not expecting any" Replied Robin."Speak for yourself" Remarked Little John. Big Brenda led the five travellers along a dimly lit hallway, up the creaky staircase and showed them to their rooms."Would not want to bump into her on a dark night" Whispered Little John. Robin grabbed him by the scruff of the neck and pushed him into his room before he had the lot of them thrown out. Everyone had a restless night apart from Little John, who could sleep through anything. Big Brenda was in the next room and was snoring profusely, which shook the whole building. Little Johns stomach had started to rumble again. Which only added to the problem.

Next morning all five were awoken by Big Brenda.

"BREAKFAST IS ON THE TABLE" She screamed at the top of her voice.

All five headed towards the dining room. Little John was already seated at the table with his elbows in the starting blocks. He was soon followed by the other four. Each of them was given a large plate full of hot tripe and haggis and a tankard full of hot steaming tea. Which looked more like treacle as it had been brewing for over two hours. All four of them, except for Little John were blurred eyed due to lack of sleep. After breakfast, all five thanked Big Brenda for her so called hospitality and shot off up the road as fast as they could. Not forgetting to wipe their feet before leaving.

Meanwhile, back in England, Prince John was still searching as to the whereabouts of Robin Hod. He had become obsessed with the matter and would talk about nothing else. The truth was that he had become very depressed regarding the whole situation. Just one story that was going round at the time, was that he tried talking to the Samaritans about his depression and paranoia. But they found him too boring and totally ignored him. He eventually travelled up to Nottingham to see the sheriff. After all, it was Robins birth place and he thought someone there must know of his whereabouts. Prince John eventually arrived at the castle gates but would soon be disappointed. A small guy on the drawbridge shouted down at Prince John.
"He,s not in"
"Where,s he gone" Enquired Prince John.
"He,s having the castle refurbished and he,s gone to look at some new carpets"
After all, the Allied carpet sale was still on.
Prince John left Nottingham even more depressed than when he arrived and travelled back to London. He left a message with the small guy on the drawbridge that he would contact the sheriff at a later date by first class pigeon post.

Back in Scotland, the five weary travellers carried on walking the Great North Road to Inverness at a faster than normal pace. They wanted to put as much distance as they could between them and Big Brenda while it was still daylight. Little Johns legs were going ten to the dozen as he tried to keep up with the other four.

"We must rest a while" Pleaded Marion.

"We can rest at the next tavern" Replied Robin.

"But that could be miles away" Said Little John.

"No it,s not, there,s one just up the road" Said Robin.

"How you know that boyo" Enquired Alan A Dale.

"I have just seen a coach party pull into the coach park" Replied Robin.

"Tavern or not, I can smell food being cooked" Remarked Little John.

Who could smell food from over five miles away. Sure enough, another mile up the road and the five weary travellers were rewarded as the Ferret Breeders Arms came into view.

The Ferret Breeders Arms was a tavern you came across by chance rather by choice. It was a tavern that was tucked away miles from anywhere. It relied on day trippers, coach parties and ramblers for its trade. It was the kind of tavern that served meals from twelve till two and bar meals from five till nine. On entering, Robin ordered five haggis sandwiches, four flagons of heavy and a half of a flagon for Marion.

"Sod off, mines a flagon like the rest of you" snarled Marion.

"Busy in here tonight" said the landlord.

Who was trying to be friendly and hospitable.
"That.s because most had received their state benefits today" replied Little John.
Who had a bad habit of saying the wrong thing at the wrong time.
"Can I have some nuts as well" asked Marion.
"Take your pick, there all in the tap room" said the landlord.
Who tried to make a joke and nearly succeeded.
Sat in the tap room were a group of ramblers, all wearing anoraks, thick woolly hats and hiking boots which looked like they were two sizes too big. The landlord laughed as he threw Marion a packet of nuts.
"Where you heading for" Enquired the landlord.
"Inverness, hope to find work with a bright spark called Mc Alpine" Replied Robin.
"Is he the guy that,s building the canal" Said the landlord.
"That,s right" Said Robin.
Robin thanked the landlord for the drinks and sandwiches and went to sit down with the others at a table which had just been vacated by a group of yet more ramblers.
"What,s that you reading boyo"
Will Scarlet had just picked up a news bulletin which had been left by one of the ramblers.
"Just thought I would have a go at the crossword in this bulletin"
"Go on then boyo, read some of the clues out"
"A type of food fish, seven letters"

"Special" Shouted Little John.
"Egg on, five letters"
"Toast" Shouted Little John. Who was thinking of food again.
"You know boyo, if you doubled your I.Q. You would have the intelligence of a decomposing turnip" Said Alan A Dale.
Little John went red in the face with embarrassment and did not say another word.
"What,s that say over there" asked Marion.
She was pointing to a large poster which was pinned to a notice board. It read.
Grand quiz tonight. A barrel of heavy for the winning team.
"Have to stay for that" Said Robin.
A few flagons later a barmaid appeared and started to hand out the quiz papers. Robin began to read out the questions.
"Which of the following numbers is the odd one out and why. 2, 7, 15, 22, 38"
"None" Replied Little John.
"Why is that boyo" Asked Alan A Dale.
All eyes turned to Little John, awaiting his answer.
"Because they can all be divided by one"
"Rubbish" Remarked Will Scarlet.
"No, wait a minute, I think it,s number 22" Said Marion.
"In fact I am certain it is 22" She insisted.
"How do you come to that conclusion" Asked Robin.

"Because if I remember correctly, there,s a chinese takeaway a few miles up the road, and number 22 is with fried rice. All the others are with chips"

"Sounds logical" said Robin. Who quickly wrote down the answer.

"Question 2, name four fruits that begin with the letter T"

"Tomato" Said Will Scarlet.

"That,s one" replied Robin.

"Tangerine is,nt it" Said Alan A Dale.

"That,s two" Said Robin.

"Tin of pears and a toffee apple. Or you could have a tapple or tommygranite"

Whispered Little John, just in case he was wrong again.

"Might as well put it down, we can,t think of anything else" Said Marion.

Little John was now grinning from ear to ear and feeling very chuffed with himself. But it was the last question that really stumped everyone."Question 499. Name three landlords that will cash a cheque"

No one could come up with an answer for that one. In fact no one could name one landlord that would cash a cheque never mind three. The quiz was over and the quiz papers handed back to the barmaid, who then handed them to the landlord to check. The winning team was announced about two hours later. It was Robins team. **"Congratulations"** shouted the landlord. As he rolled out a barrel of his finest heavy."That will keep you going for a while" Said the landlord as he shook Robin,s hand. Little John had now stopped grinning as he held out his now empty tankard. Demanding his share of the prize.
"Hang on little chap, there's plenty to go round" Said Robin.
"By the way, where are you staying tonight" enquired the landlord."Haven't really thought of it, we were too engrossed in the quiz" replied Robin."Well, I have a barn at the side of the tavern. You can stay there if you want"Robin thanked the landlord and followed him outside. Leaving Will Scarlet and Alan A Dale to follow on behind with the barrel of heavy. Quickly followed by Little John, who thought he may miss out of his share. The landlord bid them all a good night and returned to the tavern for the night."No wacky bacci tonight, especially in a barn" Said Robin to Little John.Who went red in the face as he remembered what had happened back at the Sporran Makers Arms. Alan A Dale put his hand on Little Johns shoulder and led him to one side."Have you ever heard the story of the famous

king of Wales" Asked Alan A Dale."Not sure that I have, I don,t know any Welsh kings" Replied Little John."Is this a bedtime story"He asked."No, no boyo, it,s a story with a moral to it" Explained Alan A Dale."Well boyo, this Welsh king whose name was Owain wanted to marry off his daughter see. But he did not want to marry her off to anyone. First, he had to prove he was worthy of her hand in marriage by completing a small task. Well boyo, the word got out and the news spread throughout the valleys of Wales. Hundreds of young men applied to the king for her hand in marriage because she was a real good looker see. Not only that but there was a very large dowry that went with the deal, which would set them both up for life. Anyway boyo, a long queue had formed outside the castle. The king invited the first man in and asked him if he was worthy enough to marry his daughter. The young man said that he was, so the king asked him to prove it by going to the top of the highest tower in the castle and dive off it into the moat see. The young man did what was asked off him and dived off the tower into the moat. Dead on impact was,nt he. Anyway boyo, the second young man was asked to come before the king, who asked him to do the same thing. The young chap looked up at the tower then looked back at the king and told him to take a run and jump himself. The king replied by saying O.K. Then go across the road and get me some tobacco. The young chap obeyed and was knocked down and killed by the Cardiff to Swansea express coach. So what,s the moral of the story boyo"

"Well, uhmm, look both ways before crossing the road" replied Little John.

"No, no, boyo. The moral of the story is that smoking can damage your health, is,nt it Little John agreed and went into the barn. Leaving Alan A Dale scratching his head in disbelieve.

Now I know what you are all thinking at this point of the story. You are thinking that I have completely lost the plot, that I am a complete lunatic and that I am from a different planet. The reason being that tobacco was not discovered until much later, when Sir Walter Raleigh had brought it back to England from the new world and somehow managed to singe the kings beard. This is true, as the history books tell us. But what they do not tell us is that the Vikings were in the new world long before Raleigh, Columbus, or anyone else for that matter, and they were already trading in tobacco with the Welsh, Irish, and Pics. Anyway, after that little point has been cleared up, back to the story.

Next morning and after a heavy session in the barn. Robin staggered out at an angle of 45 degrees, followed by Marion at an angle of 30, Will Scarlet at an angle of 35, Alan A Dale at an angle of 40, and Little John who had managed to keep off the Jamaican Woodbines, at an angle of 33.57 degrees. After thanking the landlord once again for his hospitality and returning the now bone dry barrel, the group set off along the Great North Road for the very last time. Just one more day and their long trek north would be over.

It was around lunch time when they came across the Chinese takeaway that Marion had mentioned the previous night at the quiz. Feeling hungry after walking all morning, they went inside and all ordered sweet and sour pork. All except for Little John, who could eat like a horse. He was the original human dustbin. He ordered two portions of fried rice, spare ribs in O.K. Sauce, chow mein with three spring rolls, and a portion of chicken lips for good measure. The secret now was to keep it down. The last thing Little John wanted to do was have a technicolour yawn in front of everyone and ruin his reputation. His face was turning white as a sheet as he was feeling a little green behind the gills from the previous night. He did however manage to keep it down but must have been feeling rough as he was quiet all day. No silly remarks, no fooling around. He just looked like a walking corps, not knowing which earth he was on, this one or fullers.

Our five travellers had been walking for over six hours and had come round from the previous nights session. Will Scarlet thought he saw a wagon about half a mile up the Great North Road which was parked up.
"It is a wagon" said Marion.
"That's right" Replied Robin.

"But there seems to be some sort of commotion going on as well" Said Alan A Dale. As they drew closer they could see that indeed it was a wagon that had been parked up at the side of the road. Harnessed to it were five heavy horses. The sixth horse was laying dead in the road. A thin guy was trying his best to get the dead horse off the road and onto the grass verge. He kicked it, pushed it, pulled it, used a few well chosen swear words, then kicked it again, swore some more then kicked it again, pushed it and whipped it. But the horse would not move an inch.
"Your flogging a dead horse there mate" Shouted Little John.
"Can you give us directions to Mc Alpines" asked Robin.
"Looking for work are you" Replied the tall thin guy.
"That,s right" Replied Robin.
"Give me a hand with this horse and I will take you there, going there myself to deliver this stone for his new scheme"
The wagon was full of large stone blocks, which the horses had a great deal of trouble pulling up the dusty road. All five went to help the wagon driver roll the dead horse off the road and on to the grass verge.
"O.K. Climb aboard aboard" said the wagon driver.

Robin and Marion sat up front with the driver. Leaving the other three to scramble up the side of the wagon where they had to sit on the hot stone, which had been under the hot sun all day. The horses were not too happy either, as they had more weight to pull and even worse, they had one less horse to do so. "Lived in Scotland all your life?" Asked Robin "Not yet" Replied the wagon driver."So how long have you worked for Mc Alpine?" Enquired Robin."about eight months" Replied the driver.He went on to explain that before driving for Mc Alpine, he was employed by the local authority. His job was to travel up and down the Scottish part of the Great North Road filling in any pot holes that he came across. He went by the name of Phil Mc Cavity.It was around tea time when Mc Cavity,s wagon pulled into Mc Alpines yard."That,s Mc Alpine,s office up there" Said Mc Cavity.Mc Cavity was pointing to a large porto type cabin high up on a hill and which over looked the whole building site as far as the eye could see. Robin thanked Mc Cavity for the ride and scrambled off the wagon, quickly followed by the others and started to walk up the hill to Mc Alpines office. All of a sudden the office door was flung open. Stood in the doorway was the great man himself. The one they called the bright spark. It was Kenneth Mc Alpine. He was a tall guy with massive shoulders, hands like shovels, red hair and a long bushy red beard. He filled the whole doorway as he was built like a bull and had the strength to match it. Stood beside him was his two faithful dogs, Whimpy and

Barrat. Now Whimpy was a bit of an unusual looking dog as he only had one ear, half of his tail was missing and he walked with a limp. This was due to getting into a bit of a scrap with a rampant ram. He also had a squashed snout due to chasing parked wagons in Mc Alpines yard. Barrat was also a little unusual as he often walked backwards shaking his head. Mc Alpine eyed Robin and the rest of the gang up and down as if he had been expecting them.

"Looking for work" Shouted Mc Alpine in his strong Glaswegian accent.

"Pardon" said Little John, who could not understand a word he had said.

It took Robin a little while to make sense of the question too.

"I said looking for work" Repeated Mc Alpine.

"That's right" Replied Robin.

"What did he say?" asked Little John.

Robin nudged him in the ribs with his elbow.

"I could do with a few more hands, especially after what's happened.

"Why, what's happened" Enquired Robin.

"You must have heard about it on your way up here" Said Mc Alpine.

"Heard what?" Asked Robin.

"The out break"

"What out break"

"The out break that,s sweeping through the whole glen"

"Yes, yes, but what out break"

"It's spreading like wild fire. People are dropping like flies"

"So you say. But what out break are you talking about?"

"The out break what I am telling you about"

"But you have not said what the out break is?"

"Sporran rash" Replied Mc Alpine.

"You will not find us going down with that. We do not ware sporran's"

" I am very pleased to hear that"

However, there was one person in the group who may contract the disease. Little John, as he once worked as a sporran makers assistant. But he assured everyone that he had been vaccinated against the disease.

"In that case you are all hired" smiled Mc Alpine.

He then shouted for one of his foremen to direct Robin and the gang to their sleeping quarters. Down at the bottom of the great glen and close to the loch were around thirty cabins which housed Mc Alpines workforce.

"You lads can have this one and the lady can stay in this one with Mc Alpines two cooks" Said the foreman.

Robin thanked the foreman and entered the cabin. Sat at a table were two lads from Yorkshire who went by the name of Winterbottom and Ramsbottom.

Now these two lads were from Dewsbury, a small market town situated in the pennines of West Yorkshire and the birthplace of that well known Yorkshire sport of flat cap chucking, which is where the idea of the frisbee came from and not from America as we are led to believe. It was also in this small market town that one of the great North of England institutions was born. The Association of Tripe and Black Pudding Makers, and which quickly spread throughout the North of England. It was in this small market town of Dewsbury that Winterbottom and Ramsbottom were employed as clog makers, but were made redundant due to cheap imports coming in from Europe. Holland to be exact.

Back in the cabin the lads were getting acquainted and swapping tales of their great trek north to Scotland.

"Have you been to Scotland before" Robin asked Ramsbottom.

"Only once. Came up to Glasgow for a laugh and went home in stitches"

It is true to say that even in those days they had a very unusual handshake in Glasgow, and Ramsbottom had the scares to prove it. The lads talked away until the early hours. Their laughter could be heard all down the glen. Little John told the tale of how he became a stuntman. Will Scarlet told tales of his many adventures while working as a pork pie salesman for Hadrian Walls, and Alan A Dale just broke into song in his funny accent.

Next morning, everyone was woken by the sound of a loud bell being rung. Little John jumped to his feet thinking he was on fire again. Alan A Dale grabbed the only coat he had and ran out of the cabin thinking it was on fire. Will Scarlet jumped through an unopened window and landed in a heap outside the cabin, and Robin who always remained calm in such situations looked for the fire bucket. Winterbottom and Ramsbottom slept on through the whole commotion.

"Where's the fire" Shouted Robin.

"Who sounded the alarm?" Shouted Will Scarlet.

As he peered through a now glassless window. Ramsbottom yawned as he lifted his head off the pillow.

"What's up, wha',s all the commotion about?" he asked.

"The fire alarm went off" Said Robin.

"That,s not the fire alarm, that,s the cook letting everyone know that foods up"

Little John made a quick dash for the canteen and was first in line to get served. As he always was when he heard the magic word. Food. He was soon followed by Robin and the rest of the lads, who were all greeted by Marion. She had been set on as the cooks assistant by Mc Alpine. The gang sat down at an empty table and was soon served the food by Marion.

"What's this?" enquired Robin.

"I don't know I only serve it" replied Marion.

"**it,s chicken**" Shouted one of the cooks from behind the counter.

"**no it's not, it's horse meat**"Shouted Robin.

"**Chicken**"

"**Horse meat**"   "**Chicken**"   "**Horse meat**""**Chicken**""**Horse meat. These two foot drumsticks are not fooling anyone**"It was like watching a tennis final as heads turned from Robin and then to the cook as the two of them continued to argue with each other. Little John was oblivious to the whole situation as he gnawed on the bone, trying to remove the last piece of meat from it and was ready to go back and ask for seconds. Robin grabbed him by the scruff of the neck and dragged him outside where he continued to shout and scream. Demanding the return of his drumstick.

"Better get off, don't want to be late on your first day" shouted Marion. Robin and the lads followed Winterbottom and Ramsbottom to the side of the loch where they were introduced to the foreman. He was a big guy in every sense of the word. He was as broad as he was tall with a well weathered face, talked with an Irish accent and only had one eye. The story goes that he was practising for the Scottish Dart,s Open, when a stray arrow bounced out of the board and took out his eye. His name was Rick O Shay. "Who,s he, some kind of mascot" He laughed. He was of course referring to Little John." Don,t worry about him, he can work all day and is strong as an ox""Only joking" laughed the foreman."Pillock" Whispered Little John."The guy fencing off the loch need,s help" Said the foreman."We will start you off there and see how you go"In charge of fencing off the whole loch was a Chinese guy who went by the name of Ray Ling. It was just before knocking off time when a shout was heard and which seemed to be coming from the bottom of the loch. Apparently, what had happened, was that Little John had been hammering in the fence post when the hammer had slipped from his hand. It plummeted to the bottom of the loch from a great height and with great speed. It only came to a sudden stop after hitting a guy on the head. Who was working at the bottom of the loch and who was in the wrong place at the wrong time.

"Why don,t you tie a piece of string round that hammer in case you drop it again and do someone a great injury" Shouted the guy that had just been hit.

"Good idea" Little John shouted back. Who then ran off to the works stores.

"How much string do you need" Enquired the store man.

"I don,t know. How long is a piece of string" Asked Little John.

"How should I know" Replied the store man.

"Easy. A piece of string is double it,s length from it,s centre to one end"

The store man was lost for words with Little Johns logic and gave him the whole lot. Back on site, Little John quickly tied one end of the string to his hammer and was soon hammering in another fence post. Once again the hammer slipped from Little Johns hand and plummeted to the bottom of the loch from a great height and at a great speed. Another shout was heard from the bottom of the loch. "I thought I told you to tie a piece of string round that hammer" "I have. Just pulling it back up now" Shouted back Little John. It is not known what the guy at the receiving end shouted back, but the air did turn a little blue. I will leave it to your own imagination as to the guy,s reply. At the end of the day, the foreman, Ray Ling turned up to inspect the days work.

"So how many posts have you managed to put in" He asked Little John

"18" Replied Little John looking very pleased with himself.

"Why only 18 when everyone else has doubled that" The foreman asked."Ah, that maybe, but have you seen how much they have left sticking out"Ray Ling just walked away shaking his head in disbelieve. Little John had got it all wrong yet again. A loud blast from a buffalo horn was heard which echoed all down the glen, and Which was a signal to all the workers that the working day was over and that the food was about to be served in the canteen. Robin and the rest of the lads were already there, tucking into their meal as Little John arrived, who soon joined them as he started tucking into his double helping, and thinking to himself if there were going to be any seconds. It was at this moment that the door was flung open and in walked Alan A Dale. Who looked really cheesed off about something. He was quickly Followed by another guy who,s head was covered In bandages after visiting the site nurse. Alan A Dale pulled up a chair and sat down with Robin and the lads as Little John had already finished his meal and had gone back for seconds."What,s wrong. You look really cheesed off " Enquired Robin. "Listen boyo. Something will have to be done about that foreman" Replied Alan.

"Why. What happened" "He has been giving me hell all day boyo" "What is it that he's done" "Well boyo. He tells me to start painting the fence, which I do see. Then he comes up behind me, slaps me on the back of the head and tells me I am putting the paint on up side down" "He,s only having a laugh and a joke with you" Said Robin. "No, no, there,s more boyo. I always sing when I am working see, and whenever I start to sing How Green Is My Valley, he joins in. He can not sing a single note right and it keeps putting me off key. Lets face it, I have a reputation to think about" "Sounds bad" Said Will Scarlet. "No, no, there,s even more boyo. He then has the audacity to tell me that I can not sing and that it is me that is singing out of tune see" Now there is one thing in life that I have learnt, and that is you never tell a Welshman that he can not sing. It causes problems. I should now as I have the scares to prove it. It was at this point that the guy with all the bandages came over and sat down next to Robin. There was something a bit odd about him and I do not mean the bandages. He seemed to be very nervous. He kept on looking up in the air, then ducking with a kind of twitching movement in between. He introduced himself to Robin and the lads. His name was Ivanhoe. Now most people do believe that Ivanhoe was just a fictional character who who was brought to life by that great author Sir Walter Scott. Once again I must say that people are wrong. Ivanhoe was indeed a real person. Ivanhoe was born and brought up in Wales. Swansea to be exact. Now I know what you are all thinking. Not another tale about a Welsh guy. Sorry, but I can not distort from the truth. From a very early age, Ivanhoe had shown a very keen interest in horticulture. This great interest into what some people may call an obsession. The truth of the matter is that he became famous through out Wales for his giant leeks. He set out like any other fruit and veg grower renting a small allotment from the local authorities. As his passion grew, he rented more and more land which he eventually bought. He was a kind of medieval Greg Wallace. Who supplied the posh hotels and restaurants with his produce. He would work long hours and at the end of each working day he would walk up the cobbled street with his hoe over his shoulder. The local people would say, there goes Ivan with his hoe. Which gives us the name Ivanhoe. His real name though was Ivan Evans. It is still a mystery why he had travelled to Scotland to work for Mc Alpine. Just one of the theories is that he lost the land due to a compulsory purchase order. The theory goes that a wealthy business man who knew someone high up in the local authority wanted to open a slate quarry. After a few exchanges of back handers he obtained the land that he wanted. Although the theory can not be proven, it is probable that this was the reason.

After Ivanhoe had introduced himself, he turned to Robin.

"Can you try talking some sense into that guy" As he pointed to Little John.

"What,s he been up to now" Sighed Robin.

Ivanhoe then began to tell Robin and the rest of the lads the whole story of how he came into contact with Little Johns hammer. Will Scarlet laughed so much when Ivanhoe came to the part regarding the piece of string that he fell backwards of his chair. Hitting his head on the next table. He suffered mild concussion. He was seen by the site doctor and remained in the first aid room for two days, under observation by a buxom nurse from the Isle of Arran.

"Good idea was that piece of string" Remarked Little John.

"Why was it a good idea when the hammer still hit me on the head" Asked Ivanhoe.

"Well, it saved me the trouble of climbing to the bottom of the loch to retrieve it"

No one said a word as they just sat there and glared at Little John, who thought that he had done nothing wrong.

Meanwhile, Big Brenda was doing a roaring trade back at the boarding house. All the rooms were fully booked due to an invasion of Sasanacs, who had flocked north of the boarder into Scotland. After all, it was the height of the tourist season. However, not all was as it seemed. There were a couple of middle aged guys who had booked in and were acting a little strange. They were always writing in little note books and constantly whispering to each other. Big Brenda had noticed this and had tried looking over their shoulder to see what they were writing about. But every time she got near they would slam their note books firmly shut. Big Brenda was getting curious and curious as each hour passed. She finally came to the conclusion that the two guys were from the English Touring Board and were going to give her boarding house a mention in one of their publications. Nothing could be further from the truth, as all hell was about to break loose. All became clear during breakfast, when one of the guys asked for some more mushrooms. Big Brenda told him to help himself and that he could find some behind the toilet door. Failing that you may find some under the toilet seat. If there is none there then we have run out. It was at this point that the two middle aged guys introduced themselves as the local health inspectors.
"I only meant that as a joke" Said Big Brenda.
"Is that so, and what joke are you trying to make about the rooms" Said one of the health inspectors.
"What,s wrong with the rooms" She asked.

"Creepy crawlies, they are all over the place"
"There were none around this morning"
"No, they only come out at night. All over the bed. They come out of the walls"
"Have you tried pulling the bed away from the wall"
"Yes, but they keep on pulling it back"
The other health inspector then butted in.
"There is also another question regarding the damp in the room"
"Which room" Asked Big Brenda.
"All of them"
"But that,s only condensation"
"So why has every room have a permanent rainbow"
"That,s only the sun light shining through the window"
"The sun can not penetrate through the window, they have not been cleaned in years"
The other health inspector then butted in.
"What about the other complaints from the guests regarding the damp"
"What complaints"
"Complaints about finding fish in the mouse traps"
Big Brenda was lost for words and had run out of excuses, but gave it one last try.
"I run a good boarding house"
"Boarding house, call this a boarding house. The place wants boarding up"
"There is only one thing for it. We will have to shut you down"

And with the final words said, Big Brenda was evicted on the spot and the boarding house was indeed boarded up ready for demolition. With nowhere to stay and no means of support, there was only one thing she could do. Travel north to Inverness in the hope that Mc Alpine would give her work.

Back at Mc Alpines everything was back to normal. That is if you could call it normal. Robin and the lads were working from dawn to dusk and Marion had just been promoted to head cook. Mc Alipine had heard the story regarding the horse meat scandal and had set up an inquiry into the whole business. He found that the two cooks were well out of order and fired them on the spot. Little John was still playing the fool and saying the wrong thing at the wrong time. He had progressed from dropping hammers from the top of the loch and dropped everything he got his hands on. If it was not nailed down, bolted down, screwed down or tied down, then Little John would find some way of dropping it to the bottom of the loch. Boxes of nails, screws, nuts and bolts, stone, bricks, planks of wood and tools, would all find their way to the bottom of the loch. In fact to tell you the truth, Little John was becoming a bit of a liability. The final straw came one morning when Little John was walking along the fence which Alan A Dale had just finished painting. He bumped into a large sign which read wet paint. The sign plummeted to the bottom of the loch and yes, you guessed it, hit Ivanhoe at the side of the head who had been in the wrong place at the wrong time yet again. It gave him yet another bruise to add to his collection. Little John peered over the side of the loch after hearing Ivanhoe screaming in great pain.

"I would take that as a sign" Shouted Little John. Who had realised what he had done and tried to make a joke of it.
"That,s right. A sign that you are a liability" Ivanhoe shouted back. The air then turned blue again as Ivanhoe used a few well chosen words, which I can not or will not mention. I will leave that to your own imagination. In view of every ones safety, especially Ivanhoe,s, Little John was given another job by the foreman. A job where he would be out of every ones way, a job where he could not get up to any mischief, and a job where it would be impossible for him to cause an accident. There was just one small problem. The foreman did not know little John very well, or the scrapes he could get himself into. He was given a sack full of candles and told to scamper up the drainage pipes which captured the water from the surrounding hills to fill the loch. The foreman wanted to know if there were any leeks or blockages in the pipes, if so, then it was Little Johns job to rectify the situation. He was the perfect choice to do the job because of his size, and anyway, what trouble could he cause up the drainage pipes. He was given a map of the network of pipes so that he knew exactly where he was in the system. But there was a problem. No one had asked Little John if he could read a map. After around an hour, and deep underground, Little John thought he could smell food being cooked in the canteen. Thinking it was nearly tea time and that he may out on second helpings if not on time. He decided it was time to come to the surface, but as he

scampered along the pipes he was in fact going deeper and deeper into the network. The problem was that Little John was reading the map upside down. It was not long before he realised that he was completely lost. His shouts and screams echoed down the whole glen and which brought everyone running out of the canteen to see what all the commotion was about. Even Mc Alpine came running down the glen to see what all the trouble was about. Accompanying him were his two faithful dogs. Barrat and Whimpy. Everyone gathered at the end of the main drainage pipe when Mc Alpine arrived with his two faithful dogs.

"What are we going to do" Asked Marion.

Who had come running up the hill side to join Robin and the rest of the workforce.

"Leave it to me" Said Mc Alpine"

Who grabbed a long length of rope and tied one end to one of his dogs, Barrat. And sent him scurrying down the pipe,

"Why Barrat when he only walks backwards" Asked Robin.

"He may not see where he is going but knows where he has come from and will know the way back out of the pipes" Replied Mc Alpine.

"Logic there boyo" Said Alan A Dale. It was not long before Barrat found Little John, who quickly tied the end of the rope round his waist and started to follow it, and of course Barrat. Little John soon emerged from the pipe none the worse for ware although a little shaken. Next day, Little John was told to work with Will Scarlet and Ivanhoe. Which did not go down too well with Ivanhoe as he became somewhat nervous and started twitching again. For every ones safety, Little John was sent to the bottom of the loch while Will Scarlet and Ivanhoe stayed at the top out of harms way. A large A frame had been erected to lower pallets of stone to the bottom of the loch. The lads on top pushed the pallets of stone off the edge and it was Little Johns job to lower them to the bottom by means of a thick rope. Easy enough thought Little John, what could possibly go wrong, as he got a firm hold of the rope. The first pallet was pushed of the edge which plummeted to the ground. The reason for this was that gravity had not yet been discovered, that did not happen until much later by that great man and another bright spark called Sir Isaac Newton. The force of the pallet coming down forced Little John to go up. In fact he took off like a rocket which had just been launched by N.A.S.S.A. Will Scarlet and Ivanhoe could only watch in disbelief as Little John flew past them at a tremendous speed. He eventually came back to earth and landed in a heap in a cluster of bushes about fifty yards away, but it was his training as a stuntman in his early years, and knowing how to fall from a great height which saved him from serious injury. Battered, dazed and bruised he slowly walked back to the loch, stating that he would not be doing that again.

Now Ramsbottom was a bit of an inventor during his spare time when he was back in Dewsbury. All the lads were looking to him to come up with some kind of device which would wake them up in the morning. Many of them would sleep in, especially if they had been on flagons of heavy the previous night. To make matters worse, Mc Alpine had started to dock the lads wages if they were late for work. After pondering on the idea for a couple of days, he came up with a solution to the problem. The idea was to throw some bread onto the cabin roof while it was still dark. Next morning as the dawn was breaking, the birds would land on the cabin roof and make one heck of a noise while pecking away at the bread. The idea worked. In fact it could be argued that it was Ramsbottom who invented the first ever alarm clock. Next morning, after being woken by the birds on the cabin roof, Robin and the lads made their way to the canteen. They were just about to go through the door when they were stopped dead in their tracks. It was if there had been a total eclipse of the sun, as half the glen was cast in shadow. Robins face turned to a kind of deathly white. He had seen this phenomenon before, and he was still having nightmares about it. Coming in through the back door after putting out some swill into the bin, which still had to develop ulcers was Big Brenda. She had arrived in Inverness the previous night and had been interviewed by Mc Alpine. She had been set on as second cook. Mc Alpine thought she would be very useful later on too, as he always had some form of charity event going on during the Scottish Darts Open. His idea was to have a sponsored walk round her. Lets face it, if Big Brenda was alive to day she would make Big Ben look like a carriage clock.

"What do you lot want at this hour" She growled.

"Breakfast" Said Little John.

"You will have to wait, it,s not ready yet" She replied.

Robin and the rest of the lads sat down at an empty table, leaving Little John at the counter, who was jumping up and down trying to see what was cooking. Big Brenda gave him a quick clip round his left ear with a hot ladle, which sent him whimpering off to join the rest of the lads. It was at this point that Alan A Dale and Ivanhoe thought there was a strange smell in the canteen. They had a nose for that kind of thing. It seemed to be coming from a large pot that was bubbling away at the back of the canteen and which Big Brenda was cooking her so called alphabet gruel in. To the welsh lads it smelt like a Turkish taxi drivers arm pit. To Little John it smelt like food, and plenty of it as well, as he already had his elbows in the starting blocks. They had not long to wait as Big Brenda appeared with a tray of steaming hot bowl,s. "What,s this" Asked Robin.

"Alphabet gruel" said Big Brenda. All the lads peered nervously into the bowl which was placed in front of them."Mine says don,t eat it boyo" Said Alan A Dale."Mine says it,s off" Said Will Scarlet."Mine says it,s swill" Said Robin."Mine says there are seconds" Said Little John.   Who had already finished his bowl and was about to go back for seconds.Robin caught him just in time and dragged him back to his chair. After explaining to him what Marion was trying to spell out to them, he turned green, went back to his normal colour then back to green again. Big Brenda was furious that the lads refused to eat her alphabet gruel as she just stood there grinding her teeth in anger. Which reminded the Welsh lads of a set of snooker balls. One was white and the rest were all colours. It was at this point that the lads decided to leave before Big Brenda boiled over. They walked slowly to the door then made a quick dash towards the loch. Leaving Big Brenda simmering on the back boiler. As the days turned into weeks, complaints were flooding in fast and furious to Mc Alpines office regarding Big Brenda,s cooking. Mc Alpine was getting a little peeved off with the whole situation. It was bad enough having to deal with his workforce dropping like flies with the dreaded sporran rash but Big Brenda and her cooking was something else. The final straw came one night when Mc Alpines two faithful dogs Barrat and Whimpy returned home one night after a night out ratting. They had been catching rats behind the canteen when they came across some leftovers which had been put out by Big Brenda. She was going to use it in one of her stews the very next day, but something must have been wrong with it because even the rats were turning their noses up at it. Barrat and Whimpy ran whimpering home and had spent the rest of the night with their paws down their throat, trying to bring up what they had previously put down. Mc Alpine was furious, and set of towards the canteen to confront Big Brenda. A brave man indeed, as it was still dark. Mc Alpine did not mince his words. He told her that never again was she to cook any food for his workforce. Instead, she would have the job of taking the packed lunches round the loch to where the men were working. He also stressed that all the packed lunches would be prepared by Marion and her assistant. Big Brenda was speechless, no man had ever talked to her like that before, especially at night. She was left speechless and just stood there open mouthed as she watched Mc Alpine disappear into the black of night.

Next morning, Marion and her assistant had been up at the crack of dawn. Marion was well into the task of preparing the packed lunches while her assistant was preparing breakfast for the lads. The birds had just started making a heck of a din on the cabin roof as they pecked away at the bread, which Ivanhoe had put out the night before, and which was a sign for everyone to raise from their slumber and make their way to the canteen. It was not long before news of what had happened the previous night reached everyone in the room. "I thought it was a little different in here this morning boyo" Remarked Alan A Dale. "How do you mean, different" Asked Little John. "Well boyo, there is more light and a lot more room see, No Big Brenda" The lads all laughed except for Little John, who could not see the joke and was already on his feet going back for a second helping. It was around 11 A.M. When once again the whole glen was cast into shadow. Even the birds had stopped singing as they thought it was night. It was in fact Big Brenda, who had just set off to deliver the packed lunches to the lads working around the loch. Strapped to her back were three massive rucksacks and in her hands were two large sacks. All containing the packed lunches, and which made Big Brenda look even more bigger and frightening than she already was. It was at this point that the greatest tragedy of all occurred during the building of the Caledonian canal.

Big Brenda was just about to reach the bottom of a steep decent which leads to the edge of the loch when she lost her footing. She rolled, bounced, then rolled again, which set off a small earth tremor. She then crashed through Ray Ling,s fencing, which was made to stop people from falling into the loch and was not designed for people like Big Brenda. She fell from a great height into the loch making a tremendous splash which echoed down the whole glen, and which sounded like six modern day depth charges going off at the same time. The guys on the other side of the loch scrambled up the steep bank to higher ground as, a tremendous tidal wave came rushing towards them. There were also reports coming in of a very large tidal wave that hit Fort William, which was quite a few miles down the loch. Big Brenda was dead on impact. Everyone came running to see what had happened."She just rolled down the hill" Said one guy who was working nearby."Tragic accident boyo" Said Alan A Dale."How are we going to get her out" Enquired Will Scarlet."What,s happened to our packed lunch" Said Little John.On hearing the news of what had happened, Mc Alpine sent six of his strongest horses to the scene which were led by Phil Mc Cavity. After a couple of lads volunteered to swim out to the body of Big Brenda and attach six ropes to her lifeless body. Robin and Mc Cavity attached the other ends to the six horses and began to pull her from the loch. The horses strained at the shear weight they were expected to pull. Even the lads took hold of the ropes and began pulling with

the horses. They were red in the face with all the effort they were putting in and did not look too happy about it. The horses did not look too happy about it either. After a few hours and with much effort, they eventually got Big Brenda on to the banking. Everyone breathed a sigh of relief. Including the horses. It was then that Robin noticed a young lad who was leaning on a shovel. He looked somewhat distressed as he was crying buckets full. Robin walked over to the young lad and to ask why he was so distressed.
"What's wrong lad?" Enquired robin.
"Big Brenda" he sobbed as he pointed to her body.
"I don,t think she felt any pain. Dead on impact I heard"
The young lad sobbed even more.
"Did you know the lass well" Said Robin as he put his arm around his shoulders.
"No. It,s not that"
"So you did not know her at all then"
"No" Replied the young lad.
"So why all the tears then"
"I am the one who has been told to bury her"
Robin left the young lad to get on with his great task with a tear in his own eye.

Now it is even said to day, that on a full moon. When the loch is calm and the surrounding hills are shrouded in Scotch mist. You may just get a glimpse of the ghost of Big Brenda, rising from the murky depths of the loch with her three rucksacks still tied to her back. Tourists from all over the world still flock in their thousands for such a sighting.

.

Meanwhile, back in England. Prince John was getting very annoyed to say the least. He was no nearer catching Robin than he was six months previous. In fact he had more chance of winning the lottery than he was of finding the whereabouts of Robin. Providing that the lottery was around in those days, which I can assure everyone that it was not. Prince John had once again contacted the Sheriff of Nottingham by first class pigeon post. As he had done on many previous occasions. The letter was picked up by one of the sheriffs servants. Who was a bit of a dimwit and had the intellect of two radish and half a turnip. The letter accused the sheriff of not using his sources to finding the whereabouts of Robin. The servant took it upon himself to reply to the letter. He stated that the sheriff probably had more sources than Prince John, and that he used them on a regular basis. He then began to list them all for Prince Johns perusal. He said that the sheriff had mint source, apple source, cranberry source, brown source, etc etc. In fact the list went on and on and filled a full sheet of parchment. On receiving the letter, Prince John flew into an almighty rage. In fact to tell the truth he went completely ballistic. He threw tankards, kicked over chairs and bounced pewter plates off the castle wall. Everyone ran for cover as he continued to rant and rave. After about three or four days of calming down, he decided to reply to the letter and accused the sheriff of loosing his marbles. This time the letter was picked up by the sheriffs secretary. A young maiden who went by the name of Dot Com. She replied to Prince Johns letter stating that the sheriff does not play marbles so how could he possibly loose them, and accused Prince John of loosing his. On reading the reply he flew into yet another rage, stating that everyone had gone mad.

Back in Paris, which is in France in case you had forgotten, Richard was still having great revues in the local press. News of his fame spread like wild fire throughout Europe. Even Mc Alpine, Robin and the lads had heard of this great superstar from Paris. But no one could even imagine that it was Richard. They had only heard of him as Larry La Rue, who was now buying at least two new frocks a week for his show. There was even talk of him doing a European tour. A good few weeks had now passed since the death of Big Brenda. The young lad who was given the job of burying her, had just about recovered although he was still having nightmares about his ordeal. The Scottish Darts Open was drawing closer by the day, but all attention was turned to that other great Scottish tradition which sadly does not exist today. I am of course referring to the annual cat racing competition. Now I would like to point out here that this event started life in good old Yorkshire. Catterick to be exact. But it moved north to Scotland as the English preferred their horse racing to cat racing. During the early days of the race being moved to Scotland. Mc Alpine owned and trained his own cat which won everything. No other cat could even come close to it. No matter what the conditions were or the length of the race, Mc Alpines cat would win. In the cat world, it was the fastest cat on four legs.

Unfortunately, like all racing cats it got too old for racing and Mc Alpine had to retire it from the cat racing scene. This really infuriated the cat as it not only loved to race but enjoyed winning as well as the fame that went with it. The cat went into bouts of depression and would become short tempered and violent. It would scour the glens to pick a fight with another cat. Sometimes if it was in a very aggressive mood it would pick fights with dogs too. The cat ended up with only one ear, half of its tail was missing, battle scars covered it,s entire body and it was blind in one eye. The problem was that the cat was far better at racing than it was at fighting and Mc Alpine re named the cat lucky. It is not known what the cats previous name was. The cat eventually died and Mc Alpine had it made into a sporran, which he wore with pride on special occasions. Robin and the lads, including Marion, decided that it would make a nice change if they all had a day out at the cat racing. After all, they had all been working from dawn to dusk and could do with a break. Even Mc Alpine agreed and offered to loan them one of his wagons and four of his best horses. He even threw in a cask of heavy for the journey. At the day of the race, everyone was up early and climbed aboard the wagon ready for the off. Marion had made a packed lunch for everyone, which would go down well with the cask of heavy which Mc Alpine had given as a kind of bonus. On arrival at the race track, they all headed for the main ring. Where all the owners and trainers were parading their cats in front of thousands of punters.

"Did anyone manage to pick up a race card for the main race" Enquired Ivanhoe.

"Yes, I did" replied Marion. As she was going through the runners of the big race.

"I just don,t know which cat to pick" She sighed.

"Just read the names out boyo" said Alan A Dale.

"O.K." Replied Marion

"Trap 1: Ginger Tom"

"Trap 2: Catatonic"

"Trap 3: Cat O Nine Tails"

"Trap 4: Cat Nap"

"Trap 5: Muted Mick"

"Trap 6: Catastrophic"

"Trap 7: Cat In Hells Chance"

"I think I will have five crowns on Ginger Tom" Said Marion.

"No, no boyo. Muted Mick will win it" Said Alan A Dale.

"How do you work that out" Said Ramsbottom.

"Carrying less weight see"

"I agree" Replied Robin.

Everyone rushed to place their bets then took up their positions to watch the big race.

All eyes turned towards the start as the trap doors sprung open, and all the cats bolted out like greased lightening.

But wait, something was wrong. There were only six runners when there were supposed to be seven cats in the race. What had happened was that Cat Nap had fallen asleep in the trap and did not realise that the trap door had sprung open. He was out of the race. The other six cats were approaching the first bend and half way round Catastrophic slipped, lost his footing and collided with Cat O Nine tails. Both cats went head over tail and crashed into the barrier. Catatonic went into some kind of trance on the back straight and was completely out of it. Cat In Hells chance had no chance and was ten lengths off the leading two cats. Ginger Tom was in the lead as he approached the home straight. But coming up fast on the outside was Muted Mick, who soon took up the lead and was first past the wining post by one length and a whisker. Some people said that he won by one length and two whiskers. Either way it was Muted Mick that had won.

"Wonder which idiot backed Cat In Hells chance" Remarked Ivanhoe.

"The name says it all" Replied Winterburn.

Little John went red in the face.

Everyone rushed to get their winnings. Except for Little John of course. Now it is not known how much they had won but it must have been a nice amount because the lads had decided to stop off at rather a posh restaurant which they had seen on the way to the race track.

The Costa Packet was the kind of place where you only visited on special occasions. The kind of place where you were expected to use the knives and forks which were provided and not your fingers. Everything was cooked to order and was served on real pewter plates and not the cheap wooden ones which Robin and the lads were used to. They even had fresh fruit on the table when nobody was poorly. There was a French chief, Italian waiter and a Hungarian violinist, who would flit from table to table while doing his fiddling. On entering the establishment, Robin, Marion and the lads were greeted by a smartly dressed guy who spoke with a posh accent.
"Have you got a reservation" Enquired the posh guy.
"Do we look like red indians" Replied Little John.
"You may just be in luck, I think we have just had a cancellation"
The posh guy then took the party to an empty table which was near an open log fire and gave each one of them a menu.
" I think I will have some of that wells fargo" Said Little John.
"You will not like that" Replied Marion.
"Why, what is it" Asked Little John.
"Snails"
"Ugh, then I think I will go for the chicken vindaloo"

Everyone else played it safe and ordered a mixed grill and placed their order with the posh guy, who quickly disappeared into the kitchen. Little Johns stomach was starting to rumble again, as it always did when he was around food.

"Why don,t you have a piece of fruit to be going on with" Said Marion.

"Good idea" Replied Little John.

Who quickly reached out to a large fruit bowl which had been placed in the middle of the table, and was brimming over with a variety of fresh fruit.

"These suede apples taste nice" Said Little John.

"They are not suede apples they are called peaches" Replied Marion.

It was at this point that Little Johns face turned red, then purple, then blue.

"There,s something wrong with Little John" said Marion.

Robin came running over while the rest looked on, not knowing what to do. Little John had eaten the peach in record time and had swallowed the stone in the middle, and which was lodged in his throat. Robin gave him an almighty slap in the middle of his back. Resulting in the stone flying across the room at high velocity. It eventually hit the bishop of Edinburgh at the back of his head, who was having a night out with one of the local nuns from Fort William. He turned towards Little John, muttered something in latin, then continued to finish his meal. It is not known what the bishop had said, but the nuns face turned bright red. I will leave you to draw your own conclusions as to what he had said. Just then, and like magic, the posh guy turned up with their order. Little John, who had now recovered, made a grab for his chicken vindaloo. The pewter plate was so hot that he dropped it and the entire contents went over Alan A Dales best tights.
"That was red hot" He screamed at Little John.
"Well it was a vindaloo" He replied.
After a bit of a clean up and Alan A Dale still ranting and raving about his best tights. Little John was brought another chicken vindaloo. But this time it was placed on the table before him.
"Why does it always happen to me boyo when you are around" Said Alan A Dale.
" It does not always happen to you" Said Ivanhoe.
"What about the incident with his hammer coming into contact with my head"
"Sorry boyo, I had forgotten about that"

It was then that Marion tried to change the conversation, and asked Ivanhoe if he had ever had a girlfriend
"Only one" He replied.
"When was that" asked Robin.
"It was back in Wales see. I was seeing this woman many years ago"
He then went on to say that it was her birthday and that he had arrived at her house with a bunch of flowers, some chocolates and a birthday card. He told her to get ready as he had booked a table for eight o clock.
"How was I suppose to know that she did not like snooker"
It was then that Ramsbottom began to tell his story.
"I had a sweetheart a few years ago back in Dewsbury. An identical twin she was"
"How did you tell them apart boyo" Asked Alan A Dale.
"One had a beard" He explained.
Just then, the posh guy arrived back at the table.
"Would anyone like desert" He enquired.
Everyone ordered a slice of backwell tart. Which soon arrived at the table.
"What are all these little white things on the top" Asked Little John.
"They are split almonds" Replied marion.
"They remind me of a chiropodists floor on a busy day" He remarked.

Everyone just glared at Little John as they had been doing all night. Wondering what he was going to get up to next. After a few more tankards of house red it was time to leave the Costa Packet and head back to Mc Alpines.

"Can we stop off at a takeaway on the way back" Asked Little John.

Everyone ignored him.

"Er, I will take that as a no then shall I"

All arrived back at Mc Alpines safely and without any further incident. Everyone helped to unharness the horses and put them in the stables, then retired for the night as it was back to work the very next morning.

At dawn, everyone was woken by the birds pecking away on the cabin roof. Everyone apart from Little John, who was still in a deep sleep. He was laying from corner to corner across the bed. His arms stretched out with his head hanging over the side. For a split second, Robin, who had gone across to wake him thought that he was dead. After a few good shakes Little John was awake.

"How do you manage to sleep like that?" He asked. "Like what?" "Spread out like a bed of dead lettuce and with your head over the edge of the bed" "Ah, the doctor said I may sleep better if I was in a fatal position" "Don,t you mean in a fetal position" "Yes, that may be the word" He replied. Little John just looked at Robin with a blank expression, jumped out of bed, dressed and ran off towards the canteen. He could smell food. Robin followed him, shaking his head and muttering to himself. The rest of the lads were already there. Tucking into some steaming hot haggis and porridge oats. After breakfast, and after Little John had finished his third helping, they all set off towards the loch. The wind was getting up and getting stronger by the minute. Kilts and sporrans were flying in a horizontal position. Little John was working away with Will Scarlet. Alan A Dale and Ivanhoe were keeping their distance between them and Little John for safety reasons. Will Scarlet was a little nervous to say the least, as he kept one eye on what he was doing and the other eye on Little John. All of a sudden, Little John stopped working and looked out to the middle of the loch. Will Scarlet also stopped working and turned to see what had caught Little Johns attention. Coming towards them was a small rowing boat with a local guy rowing like hell for leather. The two could hear him shouting something, but he was yet too far away for them to make out what he was saying. It was not long before the boat came to the shore of the loch with a loud crash. The local guy was as white as a sheet as he ran

up the side of the loch.
"What,s up" Enquired Little John.
"Beastie" Shouted the local guy.
Will Scarlet ran after the guy to try and calm him down and to try and find out what he had seen that had frightened him so much. Little John was scouring the loch to see if he could see anything. It was then that he started jumping up and down as he pointed to the middle of the loch.
"Beastie. Beastie" he shouted.
Will Scarlet turned to see what Little John was getting all excited about. In the distance he could just make out what looked like three humps floating down the loch, before disappearing into the murky depths. Robin and the rest of the lads had heard all the commotion and had all come running to see what all the fuss was about. Little John began to tell them what he had just seen.
"If it was not for the three of you seeing it then I would have said that Little John had been on the whacky bacci again"
" I thought I saw something the other night" Said Winterbottom.

"I was taking Mc Alpines dogs for a walk along the loch when suddenly they stopped dead in their tracks and started barking at something in the loch. I could not make out what it was but I did see something floating down the loch. These are the first sightings of what we call today. The Loch Ness Monster. There are many names for what they had seen. Beastie, Kelpie, and of course the Loch Ness Monster, but as I have already mentioned earlier, what they all saw was in fact the ghost of Big Brenda.

In Nottingham, the two Wassocks who Robin had the misfortune to come across had arrived there on their way back to Wessex. The biggest one, who,s voice had returned to normal after Robin had given him a swifty kick in the Trossacs and Urals, noticed one of the many the posters which had been put up around the city by the sheriff. And which offered a reward for information leading to the arrest of Robin Hod.

"That,s the guy we had seen on the Great North Road" He remarked.

"I think you are right" Said the second Wazzock.

Which is the first time the two of them had agreed on something in ages. They both made their way to the castle to inform the sheriff and of course, to claim the reward. On reaching the castle gates, the biggest of the two Wazzocks shouted up to the guy on the drawbridge that he wanted to see the sheriff, as he had news of Robins whereabouts. He quickly ran off to inform the sheriff who in turn came running to the castle gates at full speed.

"Where is he. Where is he" Demanded the sheriff.

"Where,s the reward money" Replied the Wazzocks in harmony.

"The poster states quite clearly information leading to his arrest"

"We have just given you the information as to his whereabouts"

"That maybe. But he has not been arrested yet. As he"

"That is your job not ours. If you can,t arrest him that,s your problem.

The argument went on for well over an hour. What the sheriff did not realise , is that he was trying to win an argument not just with one Wazzock but two. The sheriff had no chance of winning, and after much debate on the subject and red in the face, he finally realized that, gave them the reward money and sent them on their way. He informed Prince John by first class pigeon post. Who jumped up and down like a child in a sweet shop on hearing the news. His men were over the moon too. As Prince John seemed to be much calmer and had stopped shouting at everyone and had also stopped bouncing things off the castle wall. He summoned one of his men to saddle the fastest horse in the stable and set off at great speed to see the sheriff. On arrival, they were soon in a deep discussion as to how and when they were going to capture Robin.

"But how do we know whereabouts in Scotland he is. Scotland is a big place. He could be anywhere" Said the sheriff.

"Think about it. What,s taking place in a few weeks time" Replied Prince John.

"I don,t know" The sheriff said, with a blank expression on his face.

"The Scottish Open Darts Competition. He,s bound to be there and that,s where we will take him.

"He will have to be taken by force" Said the sheriff.

"Why is that. He should come quietly when he see,s how many men we brought"

"It,s not that. The problem is that we do not have an extradition treaty with Scotland"

"I will need twelve of your best men" Said Prince John.
"Why my men and not yours"
"Because your men come come cheaper than mine in London"
There was still another problem which the two of them had not thought of until the last minute, who was going to foot the bill for the expedition up north to Scotland. The men would need paying, food for themselves and the horses, board and lodgings, the list went on and on.
"We will put up the taxes" Said the sheriff.
"We can not do that" Replied Prince John.
"Why not"
"Because they have just gone up and are not due to go up again until next April"

Now we have always been told that it was Prince John who had taken the crown jewels and had lost them somewhere in the Wash, in Lincolnshire. The story goes that he was trying to take a short cut across the Wash and had got stuck in a bog. The crown jewels had fallen from his horse and quickly sank into the deep mud, never to be seen again. Even today, there are many treasure hunters still searching with their metal detectors trying to locate them. I am sorry to say that they will never find them as they are not there and never have been. The story is half right. Prince John had taken them but he did not loose them. He took them and put them into pawn. A kind of medieval pawn shop which can still be seen on to days high street. That is how he got the money to finance the expedition to Scotland. He never had the money to redeem them, and it is my guess that the gold was eventually melted down and the jewels were sold off to a dealer in Amsterdam. Where they were used to make other jewellery and exported all over Europe.

Now as the Scottish Open was drawing closer, dart boards were going up all down the glens, as people went darts crazy. It was one of those events that brought in thousands of visitors from all over Europe, most of them foreigners, to witness the great event. It is at this point that I would like to break away from the story as there are three points I would like to make and which I feel is relevant.

The first point I would like to make is that the game of darts was very much different to the game we know today. There were no treble twenty or double sixteen etc. The board itself was a slice of oak which had been soaked overnight in water. A target was placed over the board with the bulls eye in the middle. Each player would take it in turns to throw three arrows which were around six inches long, and try to hit the bull. Each player had ten goes and the player who hit the bull the most was declared the winner. If both players had hit the bull the same number of times, then it was sudden death. They would continue to throw until one of them missed the bull. The second point I would like to make, is that the Scottish Open used to be held in the spring time, but had to be changed to the summer. There are two reasons for this. The first reason is that there was more chance of having fine weather in the summer, as the game of darts was always played outdoors. The second reason was that the Scottish branch of the Royal Society For the Protection of Birds (R.S.P.B.) had put in a complaint to the Scottish Darts Organisation. The problem was that as everyone went dart crazy, the thud of the darts hitting the board echoed all down the glens and was putting the woodpeckers off breading. Resulting in the decline of the population.

The third and final point I would like to make is that it has always been a tradition of The Scottish Darts Organisation, to invite some kind of dignitary to present the winner of the event with the golden arrow. It was Mc Alpine himself that had the honour of this the previous year. This year it was decided by the committee to invite the one and only, Larry La Rue. An invitation was sent to him by first class pigeon post and a reply was soon received. Stating that he would be only too pleased to do the honours at this years event. After all, he was thinking of doing a few gigs in England anyway.

Back at Mc Alpines, the lads were working away. It was just before dinner time that Little John was complaining of not feeling too well. Robin told him to go and see the site nurse if he was that bad. After all, his face was a little ashen and even though it was nearly dinner time he had not mentioned food even once. Which was very unusual for Little John. Later in the day, a loud blast from a buffalo horn echoed down the glen. Which brought another end to the working day. Robin and the lads headed for the canteen. On entering, they noticed Little John sat at a table. His head in his hands and a plate of food in front of him which remained untouched.
"Still feeling rough" Enquired Robin.
Little John lifted his head from his hands, his face was drip white.

"You do look rough" Remarked Will Scarlet.
"So what did the nurse say" Asked Robin.
"She said I should see a doctor right away"
"And did you see him"
"Yes, I saw him"
"So what did he say"
"His first question was do I smoke"
"And what did you tell him. I hope it was the truth"
"I said no thank you as I have just had one before I came in"
"You idiot. What did he say to that"
"Nothing. He just gave me a funny look"
"He must have said something"
"He gave me some tablets and told me I would be on them for the rest of my life"
"Don,t worry. A lot of people are on tablets"
"Oh it,s not that"
"Then what is it your worried about"
"He only gave me seven"
"Did he say anything else"
"Yes. He asked me if my urine burned"
"And what did you say about that"
"I said I did not know as I have never tried putting a light to it"
"And what did he say to that"
"Nothing, he just gave me one of his funny looks again"
It was at this point that Robin noticed that Little John was clenching a piece of parchment in one of his hands.
"What,s that you are holding"

"Something the doctor wrote down"
"Let me see"
Robin took the parchment and began to read it.
"You idiot. The reason he only gave you seven tablets is because he wants to see you again in seven days time to see if the tablets are working"
After hearing what the doctor had wrote, the colour started to return to Little Johns face. He must have felt much better too as his food soon disappeared and was back at the counter asking for seconds.
"Why are you sat there boyo. You usually sit at the end of the table"
"The doctor also said that I should change my eating habits"
Everyone was left speechless and carried on eating their evening meal.

About ten minutes had passed when two strangers entered the canteen.
"We are looking for Little John"
The two strangers turned out to be the local sheriff and his deputy. Apparently, there had been some kind of trouble in one of the local taverns the previous night. Probably a bar room brawl. Little John was in the frame, as more often than not he was involved somewhere along the line if anything went wrong.
"I am Little John"
"Can you tell me where you were between one and two A.M. This morning"

"Yes" Replied Little John.
"Well. Where were you" Asked the sheriff.
"I was in the woods by the side of the loch"
"What were you doing in the woods at that time of night"
"I was hunting rabbits"
"Did anyone see you there"
"Yes" Replied Little John, who did not want to say too much.
"So who saw you in the woods at that time of night"
"A couple of squirrels, one owl, and a few bats"
The sheriff stood there in disbelieve at what he had just heard.
"Well the rabbits will not vouch for me as I was trying to catch them at the time"
"That,s right. I saw him coming back with a sack full of rabbits" Said Ivanhoe.
The sheriff gave Little John the benefit of the doubt and left. But not before giving Alan A Dale a caution for wearing a loud shirt in a built up area.

Next day, the lads had a day off as it was Sunday. Robin was already outside practising for the darts competition. The rest of the lads were at loggerheads, wondering what to do for the rest of the day. It is not known who had come up with the idea but it had been suggested that they all should go fishing on one of the local rivers for the day. All agreed, as it was a warm sunny day and not a cloud in the sky.

"I will go and ask Marion if she can make up some packed lunches" Said Little John.
Who was thinking of food yet again.
"What kind of fishing rod do you want. Float or fly" Enquired Ivanhoe.
"I will not need one" Replied Little John.
"I will show you lot how to catch fish"
"How is he going to catch fish without a fishing rod" Enquired Will Scarlet.
"I don,t know boyo, but he,s up to something" Remarked Alan A Dale.
Little John soon appeared with the packed lunches which he handed out to everyone, who then picked up their fishing gear and headed off towards the river.
"Just got to go somewhere. I will not be long" Said Little John.
"Where is he going now" Asked Winterbottom"
"Your guess is as good as mine" Replied Ramsbottom.
"Just leave him to it boyo" Said Alan A Dale.
"He will show up eventually" Remarked Will Scarlet.
All the lads had tackled up and was fishing away. Everyone was waiting in anticipation to see who would get the first bite and also the first fish of the day. They had been fishing for about an hour with no luck and had now decided to take a rest and tuck in to the packed lunch which Marion had prepared for them earlier.

"I wonder where Little John is" Enquired Will Scarlet.

"He will soon turn up when he smells food" Replied Ivanhoe.

Everyone laughed and continued chatting away as well as enjoying the packed lunch.

"Have you ever fished before boyo" Alan A Dale asked Ivanhoe.

"I used to do a lot of fly fishing back in the valley,s" He replied. "Did you catch anything big" "Once caught a three pound bluebottle" Everyone broke into laughter once again "There,s Little John" Someone shouted. The lads all turned to see Little John just coming into view over the brow of the hill. He was heading for the river bank about fifty yards from where the rest of the lads were. He seemed to be carrying what looked like a crate of bottles and had a large sack thrown over his shoulder. Now as the theory goes. Gunpowder was discovered in China, and rightly so. It was Ray Ling who had brought some barrels of the stuff over to Scotland to blast out the large rocks within the loch which the pick and shovel brigade could not shift. However, there were two problems. The first problem is that Ray Ling had not heard the reputation of Little John. The second problem was that Little John and gunpowder was like oil and water. They just did not mix. It was Little Johns idea to fill the empty bottles with gunpowder, tie a rock to the bottle, put in the stopper including the fuse, light it and toss it into the middle of the river. The bottle would then explode and bring the fish to the surface. A good idea you may think and you would be right. The thing is that we are talking about Little John and something has to go wrong if he is involved, and it did. The first mistake was to give him access to the gunpowder in the first place. The second was that he put too much gunpowder in the bottle. The third mistake was that he did not secure the rock to the bottle in the right way. As he tossed the bottle into the middle of the river, it sank for a few seconds then came to the surface as the rock had come away from the bottle. Little John saw the danger and quickly ran down the river bank instead of running up it and putting as much distance between himself and the bottle, which was catching him up with every second. All of a sudden and without warning there was a tremendous explosion and a thick cloud of thick dense smoke rose into the sky. The force of the blast knocked the lads off of their feet. As they picked themselves up they ran towards Little John with their ears still ringing from the blast. They found him covered in glass, soaking wet and shaking like a leaf in a gale force wind. Will Scarlet told him a few choice words. Ivanhoe said nothing as he was already on a short fuse because not only had little John nearly blown himself up but had scared all the fish who had swam to deeper water in the loch for cover.

"Well. That,s just ruined a good days fishing" Said Ramsbottom.

"There,s only one thing for it boyo. Let,s head for the local tavern"Said Alan A Dale.

And with that the lads headed off. Leaving Little John to make his own way home and explain to Mc Alpine and Ray Ling how the tremendous explosion came about and which was heard for miles around.

Larry La Rue or should I say Richard, had left Paris and had made the crossing over the English Channel to England. After receiving V.I.P. Treatment from the custom officials and clearing boarder control, set out towards London. Where he would connect with the Great North Road to Scotland. The going was heavy as the rain was pelting down. The weather man had got it wrong again. Prince John had left London the day before, after putting the crown jewels into pawn somewhere on the Kings Road. He travelled up to Nottingham to meet up with the sheriff and his men. After packing some supplies into a large wagon which was pulled by two oxen, they set off on the Great North Road. They had only been on the road for a few hours when a thick dense fog came down and visibility was at a minimum.
"I think we have taken the wrong road" Said the sheriff.
"Why do you say that" Replied Prince John.
"I have just tripped up over a gravestone and there are no cemetery,s around here"
"Is it anyone you know" Enquired Prince John.
"No. Someone called miles from London"
It was not long before a strong breeze got up and the fog cleared. Everyone could see that they were still on the Great North Road which stretched out in front of them.

Back at Mc Alpines, the days had turned into weeks and the great day which everyone was keenly awaiting was upon them. It was the eve of the Scottish Darts Open. Robin was getting his final practice in, as too were the many others who were going to compete for the coveted golden arrow. The great glen echoed to the constant thud of the darts well into the night. Little John had been very quiet and secretive for the past couple of days. He was up to something as all he would say is that he was going to win the competition this year. Everyone was trying to guess as to how he was going to achieve this as no one had even seen him practice for the great event. All anyone could get out of him was that no one would even come close to beating him and that he would be declared the outright winner. He was definitely up to something with all the bragging he had been doing. Everyone was on edge. Especially Ray Ling, who was now keeping a constant check on his supply of gunpowder. Next morning, everyone was up early for the great day ahead. Marion had done some packed lunches, Mc Alpine had loaded a barrel of heavy onto the wagon, Alan A Dale was wearing his pink shirt with grey tights and robin was dressed in lincoln green. Everyone headed up the hill to where Mc Alpine was putting the final touches to his four horses which would be pulling the wagon. They looked magnificent. Mc Alpine had put on his best kilt and his special sporran which was made from his pet cat lucky.Everyone wished Mc Alpine a good morning as they climbed aboard the wagon.

They were soon on their way to the great event. They had travelled about five miles down the road when Mc Alpine said he had to make a small detour as he had promised to pick up a friend on route. He had only gone about a mile down a side road before pulling up in front of a small cottage with a thatched roof. He was greeted at the gate by his friends sister, who informed Mc Alpine that Ethelred was unready."Will you take some tea" She asked."Don,t want to put you to so much trouble, we will just have half a cup" After drinking their tea, Ethelred was still unready and they had to leave without him. It was mid morning when Mc Alpine pulled into the wagon park, which was filling up by the minute. Hundreds had arrived before him and there were still hundreds more yet to arrive. Robin and Little John climbed down from the wagon and ran off to register for the big event. The others mingled in with the crowd and began looking at the mass of stalls which seemed to stretch out for miles. Marion had heard that there was one particular stall that was selling bags which were made from real crocodile skin. But by the time she found the stall the bags had been snapped up. The next stall down was run by old Agnus and her husband Jock. They had been married for over thirty years and there was nothing that Agnus would not do for Jock and nothing that Jock would not do for Agnus, and that is exactly what they did for each other. Nothing. Now Agnus and Jocks speciality was their home made rhubarb pies which they sold each year at the Scottish Open. They were two inches wide and twelve inches long and went down well with the mass crowds. Helping them out on the stall was their only son, an ugly looking lad that did not get out very much. In fact he was even uglier when he was a baby. If he had been born in the modern world, then I suspect that his incubator would have had tinted glass. Most people believed that he was conceived on the Great North Road. The reason was that it was where most accidents happen. He was also a little dim witted. The light was on but no one was at home. One rumour that went round was that because the lad was so ugly Agnus had developed morning sickness after he was born. Yet another rumour was that Agnus must have been a champion weight lifter to have carried a dumb bell around for nine months. Agnus was a little cheesed of with him today though, and that is putting it mildly. On their way to the Scottish Open, she asked the lad if he had remembered to feed the cat before they left. He replied that he had and that he had fed it to the dog next door. What he did not tell her was the fact that the cat had killed the dog as it got wedged in the dogs throat and the dog owner was not very pleased about it. There was obviously trouble brewing for her when she returned home. A couple of stalls down was a stall which was selling cup cakes and buns. It was run by two sisters, Donna and Kebab. There were also stalls selling tankards, home made jewellery, Rugs, Tapestries, antiques and antiquities and a variety of other wares. There was a caber tossing competition, strongest man competition, a demonstration on sporran making and even a ferret race. With all this going on and plenty to see and plenty to do, it was a grand day out for all the family. One of the main attractions and which had proved very popular year after year. Apart from the darts competition of course, was the grand prize draw. Now this prize draw had a bit of a twist to it. Everyone who had paid the entrance fee to watch the Scottish Open was issued with a piece of parchment with a number written on it. During the day, six numbers were pulled from a hat and the six people who had one of the matching numbers, competed against each other to determine an outright winner. Each one threw three darts, three times at a target and the one that got the bullseye the most, or nearest to it was declared the winner. He or she then went on to the prize board where they could win various prizes. This prize draw was repeated three times throughout the day, so if your number was notpulled out from the hat the first time, then you still had two more chances of winning. The prizes were more or less the same year after year. For example, there was usually a chastity belt, a left handed tankard, a kilt with matching sporran, a set of spare keys for the chastity belt. Which could be worth a small fortune to the guy that had won the chastity belt previously. There was also a new invention that could be won. A trouser press. No folks, it is true and you did read it right. They really did have trouser presses in the medieval times. They consisted of two thick planks of wood and three heavy rocks. I will leave it to your own imagination as to how it was used. There was also the star prize if you could hit the bull. This was usually a covered wagon or a small rowing boat. All three prize draws were overseen by a guy called Tim Rowan and his side kick Tony White.

It was not long before a blast from a large buffalo horn was heard which signalled that the dart competition was about to start. Robin had a bye in the first round as the guy he was suppose to play was competing in the caber tossing competition earlier on in the day, and had come down with a very bad dose of caber tossers elbow. Little John on the other hand had been disqualified. The reason, and much to the amusement of the crowd. Throwing three hedgehogs.

"So that was his secret" Said Will Scarlet. "How did he think he would get away with that boyo" Replied Alan A Dale. All just shook their heads in disbelieve. Robin sailed through the next few rounds and reached the final. He had not missed the bull once in his quest. It was announced by a fat guy with a loud voice, that Robin would play a Scottish salmon fisherman who went by the name of John West in the final match. A deadly silence fell on the crowd as the fat guy tossed a groat into the air to determine who threw first. It would be John West. The crowd waited with baited breathe as West threw his first arrow. It was a bulls eye. His second throw was also a bulls eye followed by a third. Robin followed suit and threw three bulls eyes. This went on until the final throw when West threw two bulls and his third arrow was just outside the bull. All that Robin had to do was to throw three bulls eyes to win the competition and the coveted golden arrow. You could hear a pin drop as Robin took aim. Thud, the first arrow was just off centre but was still a bull. Thud, the second arrow was dead centre and the third split the shaft of the second arrow but still counted as the bulls eye. Robin had won and a deafening cheer rose up from the crowd. The fat guy with the loud voice declared Robin the winner and beckoned him to come forward to take his prize. Not far away and watching the whole event was Prince John and the Sheriff of Nottingham.

"Shall we take him now" asked the Sheriff"

"No. Wait until he takes his prize, then we will have both" Replied Prince John.
"Good thinking" Said the Sheriff.
It was at this point that another loud blast from the buffalo horn blasted out, and the fat guy with the loud voice introduced the famous Larry La Rue on stage to present the golden arrow. Or should I say Richard the Lion Heart, who pranced his way to the middle of the stage with much approval of the crowd. Robin accepted his prize and held it aloft as yet another loud roar went up from the crowd.
"**TAKE HIM**" Shouted Prince John.
The Sheriff and his men rushed forward only to be confronted by Robins men. Another almighty brawl ensued in front of the stage where a bottle of heavy was thrown by some unknown person in the Scottish crowd and which struck Richard on the head, where he collapsed in a heap. He soon recovered and got to his feet.

"Where am I, and why am I dressed like this" Said Richard.
Who rushed off the stage to dress in more appropriate attire. He quickly returned on stage as the brawl continued.
"**STOP**" Shouted Richard.

Prince Johns jaw dropped open as he now recognised his brother and ordered his men to yield. The smack on the head from the bottle of heavy had brought back Richards memory. He now knew who he was and had no recollection of the famous Larry La Rue. Which I suppose is a good thing in some respect. Both Robin and Prince John were ordered to Richards tent. Robin began to explain how he had been kicked out of the Federation of Master Builders and forced to flee to Scotland to seek work. The situation was soon rectified as Richard ordered the F.M.B. To reinstate him. The order was sent by first class pigeon post. Outside the tent there was a deadly silence. Mc Alpine had got on stage and had just announced that he was abandoning his project on the Caledonian Canal. His reason was that he could not find the men to complete the project due to the outbreak of sporran rash which was spreading like wildfire. As he was one of the largest employers in the area the news came as a great shock to many people. "Well boyo, I suppose I could go back to singing in the bars" Said Alan A Dale."But what about the rest of you.It is believed that Mc Alpine had given Ivanhoe a plot of land to start growing his fruit and veg, which he sold to the many bed and breakfast establishments as well as hotels, which were springing up all over Inverness, as new industry had just been born in Scotland, tourism. People were flocking in their thousands to see if they could get a sight of the ghost of Big Brenda. Richard too helped out as he imposed a trade ban on the import of cheap clogs arriving from Holland. Making the way clear for Ramsbottom and Winterbottom to return to Yorkshire and start up their clog manufacturing business. Will Scarlet went to work for Ivanhoe as a delivery man as his business expanded. Fryer Tuck continued to run his greasy spoon near Scotch Corner, as well as dodging the food and hygiene inspectors from the local authority. It is believed that Robin sold the golden arrow to a bullion dealer and ended up in Yorkshire where he started his own building business. It is also believed that Marion and Little John went with him. Richard forgave his brother Prince John, after all , blood is thicker than water. However, he did warn him to keep his hands off the crown of England. Richard returned to France where he lived out the remainder of his life in luxury. Prince John did eventually become king of England after Richards death. But only after being forced by the barons of England to sign the Magna Carta at the bottom. But that is another story.

Printed in Great Britain
by Amazon